BABY

CLOWN

For C. B., the original B. C.
K. L.

To Clara, the youngest performer in the Cordell circus
M. C.

Text copyright © 2020 by Kara LaReau
Illustrations copyright © 2020 by Matthew Cordell

First edition 2020

Library of Congress Catalog Card Number pending
ISBN 978-0-7636-9743-3

20 21 22 23 24 25 CCP 10 9 8 7 6 5 4 3 2 1

Printed in Shenzhen, Guangdong, China

This book was typeset in Filosofia.
The illustrations were done in ink and watercolor.

Candlewick Press
99 Dover Street
Somerville, Massachusetts 02144

visit us at www.candlewick.com

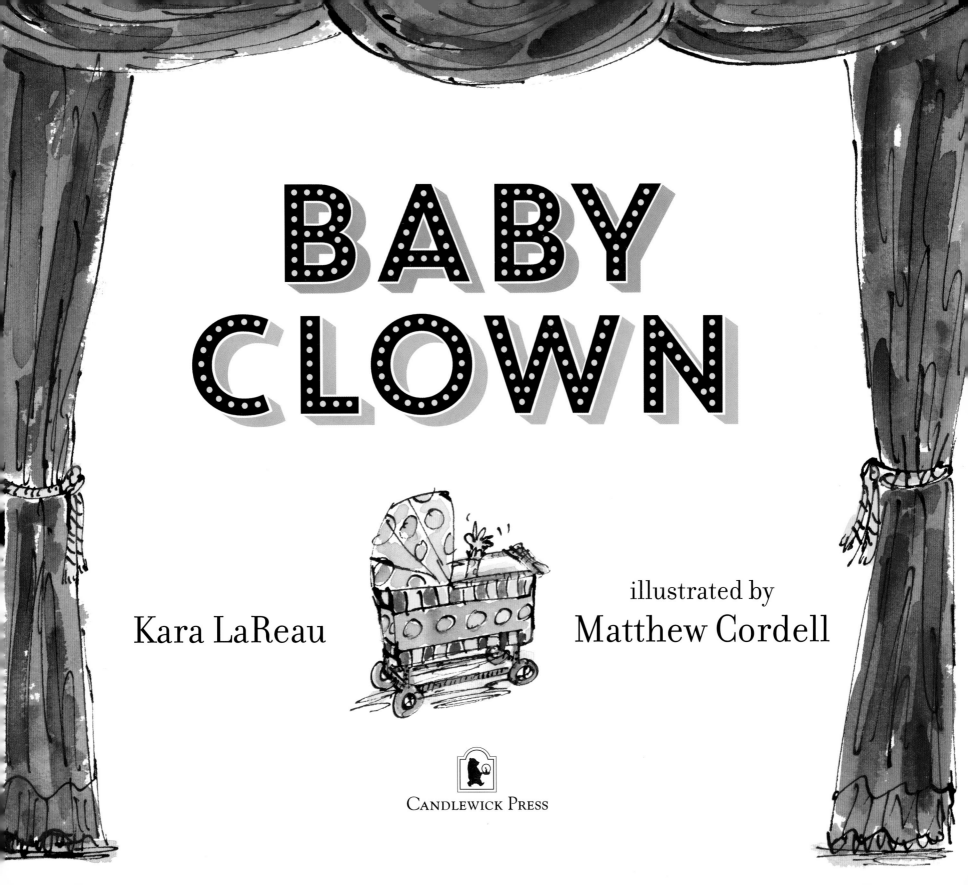

BABY CLOWN

Kara LaReau

illustrated by Matthew Cordell

CANDLEWICK PRESS

When Boffo and Frieda Clown had a baby,
everyone in the circus was over the moon.
"A STAR is born!" said the big boss, Mr. Dingling.
"We'll call him Baby Clown."

There was just one problem. Baby Clown was not a very happy baby.
He cried all the time.

"Somebody'd better cheer up that baby," warned Mr. Dingling.
"My clowns do not wear frowns!"

Boffo and Frieda tried everything.

They fed Baby Clown when he was hungry

and burped him when he was gassy

and changed his diaper when he was poopy

and rocked him when he was sleepy.
But still, Baby Clown cried.

WAAAAAH!!! WAAAAAH!!! WAAA

The Clowns tried juggling.

They tried driving around in their tiny car.

They tried making their silliest clown faces.
But still, Baby Clown cried.

WAAAAH!!! WAAAH!!!

The Clowns asked for help from the other performers.

The trapeze artists tried.

Then the animals tried.

Even the wire walker tried.

But still, Baby Clown cried.

WAAAAH!!! WAAAH!!! WAAAH!!!

"Maybe he doesn't want to be a clown," said Boffo.
But when he and Frieda tried to remove Baby Clown's red nose and
jaunty hat and striped pants and big shoes, he cried even harder.

"What is *wrong* with that baby?" asked Mr. Dingling. "There is no room for crying in my circus!"

"We've tried," said Boffo.

"And we've tried," said Frieda.

"And we've tried, and we've tried, and we've tried," said the other performers.

"Well, keep trying," said Mr. Dingling. "The show must go on!"

That night, the circus was sold out. The crowd thrilled to see the trapeze artists

and the animals on parade and the death-defying high-wire act.

But Baby Clown was not thrilled.

"Oh, no," said Frieda.

"What should we do?" said Boffo.

"The show must go on," Mr. Dingling said.

He walked out to the center ring and shouted into his megaphone,
"And nooooow . . . the newest addition to the Dingling Circus . . .

!!! WAAAH!!! WAAAH!!!

BABY CLOWN!"

Everyone in the circus held their breath
as everyone in the audience looked at Baby Clown.

And that's when Baby Clown had a *full-blown meltdown*.

WAAAAH!!!

WAAAAH!!!

WAAAAH!!!

He wasn't a clown anymore, or even a baby.
He was just a big, wide, loud mouth.

But the audience didn't mind at all.
They thought Baby Clown's meltdown was part of the act.

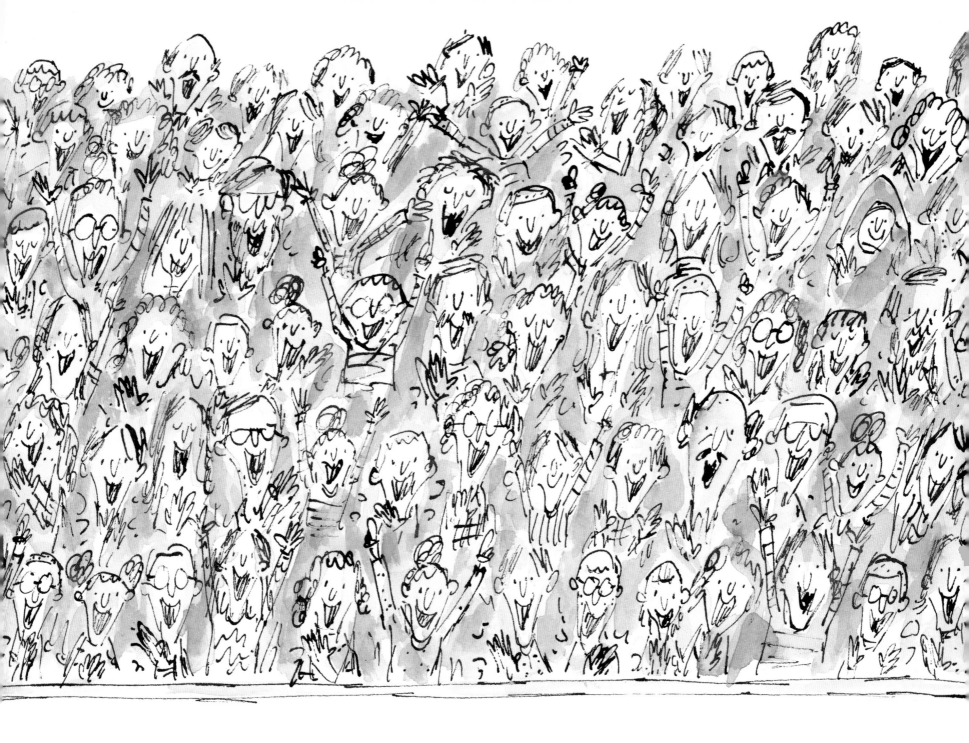

In fact, they clapped louder than they ever had before.
"Hooray!" they cheered. "Hooray for Baby Clown!"

And what did Baby Clown do? For a moment, he stopped crying.
As he looked around at the clapping, cheering crowd, his teary eyes grew wide.

His lip trembled.
His mouth opened.
And then . . .

"Hee-hee-hee!" Baby Clown giggled, clapping his own hands.
And then he made his very own silly clown face!

Everyone in the circus sighed.

"All he needed was *applause*?" said Boffo.

"Now, *that's* funny," said Frieda.

The Clowns gave their baby a happy (and relieved) hug.

Then the whole Clown family gave the crowd their silliest clown faces,
and the crowd gave them a well-deserved standing ovation.
"Hee-hee-hee!" Baby Clown giggled again.

"Just as I thought," said Mr. Dingling.

"A STAR IS BORN!"